The
By

The
Land
Of
Fall

To my family and friends: you mean the
world to me.

The Land of Fall

**And Other Stories of
Pumpkin Jack
and His Friends**

There are a few contributors to my
life that I'd like to thank.

William Osborne for giving me ideas and
encouraging me to write, Adom, for teaching
me what love is, Bastet, for teaching me how
to start over, Jessica for reading my
scribbling, Jessica for the artwork gracing
the cover, and Kay Ostu for inspiration on
the last story.

And finally and most importantly, Tisha and
Steffany, for without whom the Land would
never have existed at all. There is a Land for
all of us, somewhere out there in our hopes
and dreams and I hope I've given you a
ticket to go visit your own.

Table of Contents

Foreword:

These tales are tales I made up for my kids when they were young. I started with the basic idea and as they would ask questions (some of which are quoted in the book), I would fill in more and more details.

The idea of writing them down hung around for a decade or so. Then finally I remembered that I wanted to put them into written form for my kids and for others to enjoy as well.

The Island is indeed a mythical place and not just because it's always fall there. It says in the manuscript that the location is "just off the coast" but it never says just which coast. The original is an English-speaking country but there are plans in process to translate the book and the individual stories into Spanish and French and possibly Hebrew or Arabic.

That lack of location is not an accident. I wanted anyone who reads the stories to feel that they could be written about an Island off of their coast as well.

Enjoy.

Pumpkin Jack
And The Fountain

The Green Man

So... once upon a time, there was a Green Man. Now, I know, most stories nowadays do not start with "once upon a time" but as you will see, this story is not going to be like most stories. That is because it was told to me by the Green Man.

Now, he wasn't called the Green Man because his skin was green, because it wasn't, and he wasn't called the Green Man because his eyes were green, because they weren't.

He was called the Green Man, because wherever he went, wherever he was spotted, whatever he did, he always wore green. Green shoes, green pants, green shirt, an old faded green coat, and an even older, even more faded green floppy leather hat.

I met the Green Man in a coffee shop downtown where I go sometimes to write and watch the world go by. I met him there and after we became friends, I met him and talked with him many times. He never wore any color but green and he always drank green tea instead of coffee.

The first time I saw him come in, he noticed me sitting there writing and sat down at my booth to ask me what my writing was about. That started a long term conversation over many cups of coffee and tea about his stories about the Land of Fall.

He never said much about anything else, including himself, actually. The only other thing I ever knew about him was that he liked music.

Whenever an ice cream truck would drive by or whenever someone would occasionally play a song in the shop's ancient jukebox, he would stop for a moment, and listen with his eyes closed, and just nod, and then open his eyes again and go on with his stories.

Now, the Land of Fall, what a place that is! With villages with names like Pumpkindale and Scarecrow Corners and Turkeytown, and people like Pumpkin Jack and Freckled Moley and The Mary Who Wouldn't and Mr. Boot and Turner Jake.

It was all fascinating to me. I just listened to his stories at first but then got the idea to write them down, writing as fast as I could. I didn't get them all, but I did get most of them.

I'll start out with the same story he started out with, the story of Pumpkin Jack and the Fountain.

Pumpkin Jack and the Fountain

Just who is Mayor Jack?

Of course, if you are reading this story, then you would be asking yourself that question, wouldn't you? Who is he? What is he mayor of? How did he get that way? And other such questions. "Aha", you say to yourself, "but I'm asking the questions and you don't seem to be giving any answers!" Doesn't seem quite fair, does it?

And of course, the first rule of storytelling is to be fair to the listener; well, not the first rule, but we're not here to get caught up in dangling verbs and sentence parts like some English grammar test. Oh, no, we want the story, don't we? So here you go.

Mayor Jack was called that for two very good reasons. One is that he was, of course, the Mayor. The Mayor of what? Why, of Scarecrow Corners, of course. Can it be? You say you've never heard of Scarecrow Corners? How about Pumpkindale? Or Turkeytown? Or even, perhaps, you've never even heard of the Land of Fall?

Oh, my friend, it seems you're in for quite a time. In order to explain what and who Mayor Jack is, I must explain Scarecrow Corners; and in order to explain that little town, I must indeed tell about the Land of Fall.

First of all, the Land of Fall is not really a 'Land', as most people would think of it. It's more of an Island, just off the coast of the mainland. Now, there are two ways to get to this island (assuming, of course that you are human and not of the winged or finned sort of creature); that being by water and by train.

Traveling by water would seem to be the least common or safe of the two. You'd have to deal with tides and winds and hungry flapping seagulls and people getting quite ill, being this is usually their first time on board and Captain, could you please hand me that buck-... well, you get the idea.

Coming to the Land of Fall would be an adventure. Not the sort where you have pirates and parrots and skeletons singing odd songs and the much-repeated sound of flapping sails, but an adventure, nonetheless.

And you'd think that the train coming to the island would be safe, calm, quite comfortable, the sort of drowsy ride where you'd wake up and stretch and rub the sleep out of your eyes and ask your traveling companions, "Oh, are we here already?", that sort of ride.

But if you thought that about the train for the Land of Fall, whoo, boy, I'd not put much stock in your

picking the winners of horse races or
even frog races for that matter.

You see, the train which comes
to the Land of Fall is quite different
than the other trains people use today.
It's pretty old, for one thing, running
on steam and coal instead of the shiny
electric trains that everyone seems to
want to ride on to travel quickly here
and there. And it's only got three parts;
the cab or engine, a passenger car, and
the caboose.

Now, which would you think to
be the most important car? If you said
the engine compartment, you're
technically correct. Because without
such a thing, of course, the whole train
won't move. Lots of people's schedules
would be thrown off, there would be
much grumbling and muttering under
one's breath and looking repeatedly at
one's watch which, as any younger
person knows, will not Help The

Situation. Adults do tend to think differently, you know. But you'd be wrong.

If you said the caboose, you'd be wrong again, because the caboose is there to... well, it's... well, it's there to something; no one knows just quite what.

But the passenger car, now, that's a different thing entirely. For the passenger car is usually filled with passengers. Seems logical enough, you say, but not everything in this story (or most good ones, for that matter) is based on logic, or what people think should be, but what is.

The passengers on the train to the Land of Fall (which we explained earlier, was an Island Sort Of Land), are not your ordinary, run-of-the-mill, briefcase-carrying, watch-tending sort of passengers, oh, no. They come with a purpose.

What's the purpose, you might inquire? Oh, it varies from person to person; let's take a run through the car today and see who's there.

It's an almost empty train car with only three passengers. First of all, there's Mayor Jack. He has light blue eyes and a clean-shaven face with a crooked nose due to a pelican accident when he was younger and crab-fishing for a living. He's fairly spry four his stoutness of body and looks and acts younger than the five decades or so he has spent upon the Island. He had to head to the mainland to get something for his wife for her birthday, which as any good husband knows (and Mayor Jack is indeed a good one) must be something bought from away.

It cannot be just something he bought when he wandered down to, say, the local hardware store. Nor even the odds-and-ends shop that old Aunt

Corrinne runs in her place at the tail end of Scarecrow Corners, even though the sort of Stuff that you find in Aunt Corrinne's shop usually can't be found anywhere else. He must go to the mainland to get it.

The next passenger on the train today is Mr. Arthur P Gonfrey, the Third. Now, Arthur P., as he likes to be called, looks the part of someone with "the Third" after their name. He wears those biggish, round wire-rimmed glasses, a serious (as if there ever was another sort of variety for him) mustache of inciting-envy-in-walruses proportions, a very ample waistcoat to allow for his very ample waist and a newspaper kept tucked so carefully at Just The Right Angle and appears as if "harrumph!" were his standard greeting for everyone he meets.

This might lead a person who has been brought up around similar Arthur P's to think of him as some sort of straight-laced, stuffy person who grumbles a lot and is Not So Good with children.

However, Arthur P is the history teacher in the school at Scarecrow Corners. He is well known in the Land for his love of a good story or joke, even if he is the one it's being played upon. He has a habit of starting a story and winding into it most eloquently in his classroom with every child rapt in their listening when the sudden chime of the class bell tell them that, sadly, they must put off finding out the end of the Big Mouthed Frog or the Raisin Pie story for another day. The twinkle in his eye should let any alert person know that here is someone who knows how to play jacks or climb a tree or comfort a stuffed animal injured in The Desk Wars or make a fort where he will make a Last Stand Against The Ravening Hordes.

The third and final passenger today is Turner Jake, Mr. Boot's assistant. His name is actually Jake Turner, but he is not only the assistant at Mr. Boot's book store in Turkeytown, he's also the fastest reader on the Island. The kids say he can read as fast as you can flip the pages, which is why they flipped his name around. He's skinny, has a skinny long ponytail and a skinny long beard and a skinny long face, usually half-hidden by a baseball cap. Turner Jake is by far the oldest inhabitant of the Island and seems to have been around since the beginning of it when the villages were just forming.

Mayor Jack is the most important person in our story today. He is, after all, Mayor Jack of Scarecrow Corners. Scarecrow

Corners is the largest village in the Land of Fall, not to be confused with other Corner villages which have only one or two corners, and not very Corner-ish ones at that.

It has electric street lamps and even a large white marble round fountain in the town square, usually used by horses as a sort of drinking fountain. It is also used by children on a warm day to look for pennies and wonder whether their goldfish would like the pond (most don't).

Yes, horses. There are no cars allowed on the Land of Fall, mostly because it's a small place and you can usually walk from one part to another within a goodly amount of time. It is also because cars tend to be rather smelly and cause people to rush about fastly here and fastly there and no one is interested in doing anything fastly on the Island, thank you very much.

There are other villages, of course, in the Land of Fall; it wouldn't be much of a Land with only one village, now would it? There are the villages of Pumpkindale and that of Turkeytown but they are smaller than Scarecrow Corners and do not fit into our tale today.

"Jack", of course, is not the Mayor's real name, any more than the President's is "Mr. President" or a doctor's real name is "Doctor". It is just that that's his title, sort of like "Your Majesty" for a queen or "His Excellency", for a Duke, if this were some sort of story of times long ago. So everyone calls him "Mayor Jack" or just "Jack", if you are on more familiar terms with him. Most people call him that since he seems to be on good terms with everyone on the island.

Mayor Jack has been a man and Mayor Jack has been a woman.

Mayor Jack is the title that the people who live on the Island give to the mayor of Scarecrow Corners and it comes from the story of Pumpkin Jack and the Fountain.

Now that we've explained who and what Mayor Jack is, perhaps we'd better explain something about this Land he's the mayor of. The Land of Fall gets its name from a very simple thing; it is almost always Fall there.

Oh, there is a quick spring with flowers blooming, there's a short summer that lasts about a week and there is a week or so of snow at the end of fall, but that usually doesn't last any longer than a few days, itself. Being of a different nature than the mainland, there are, of course, different ways and methods of doing things upon the island.

For example, there's no summer vacation from school, since

there's not much of a summer. The schools' schedules and other holidays are also affected by it. There is no Labor Day or Memorial Day or Boxing Day, like in Canada.

"OH!" a school-age child might reply in dismay, "No summer vacation?" But wait, don't be too sad. Each class of students in the school at Scarecrow Corners takes off an entire week for Halloween and the same amount of time off for Thanksgiving.

Halloween always happens on a Friday, and the school always holds a lively costume party and parade for it. Thanksgiving is always on a Saturday, being that most of those who cook the Thanksgiving meal need some time to prepare it.

The children living on the Island didn't used to take off so much time for school, usually just a day or two if that much. It was study, study,

study till the words seemed to leap off the page into your brain and fly around there like so many pigeons disturbed by a cat.

But the Pumpkin Jack, not one of long long ago, but the father of this one, the present one sitting on the train, the current holder of that position, was very instrumental in bringing about the celebration of Halloween as the children of the Land of Fall know it today, with all the costume parties, candy, apple-bobbing, hay rides and all sorts of things associated with it.

Where do I start? Where every good story starts, I suppose...

Once upon a time... no, really, it did start out that way, the story did, and I'm not one to change some part of a story just because it's not the Most Modern Thing, or because a lot of other stories start differently than that.

So, as I said, once upon a time, the seasons didn't change much in the Land of Fall as we've already discussed. Oh, yes, spring would bring the rains for a week or so, the hot days would come with ice cream and cotton candy, and the kids would slide down the hill on the snow behind the schoolhouse in Scarecrow Corners.

But those only lasted a few days or so, each one, and the season of fall in the Land of Fall went on for months; the chilled mornings, frost barely showing on the windowpanes; the dry, colorful leaves that covered the sidewalks and dusty lanes between the villages; the tangy smell of hickory and birch tree wood fires filling the air.

This particular story about Pumpkin Jack and the Fountain takes place at the beginning of the fall season.

You see, the Fountain in question was not just any old fountain. It was a big fountain in the middle of the square in the middle of Scarecrow Corners and it was a famous fountain.

People would throw coins in it, horses would drink from it, and young boys would take off their socks and shoes and roll up their pant legs to wade in it and threaten to throw their sisters in it.

It was a fountain shaped in a wide circle, with a spout in the center that made it look like a big birdbath with the water coming from its top.

It was built long ago almost from the time the first town in the building was built. It was made of white marble and it glistened in the sun as fresh as the day it was made.

The Pumpkin Jack in this case wasn't even the mayor. He was the first Jack. His name was Jack, and when he was a young boy, the town had not yet gotten around to naming all their mayors Mayor Jack.

The story of Pumpkin Jack and The Fountain doesn't just involve Jack, though. It also involves his sister, his friends, his parents and most of the people in the town, especially the children.

In any case, this story is mostly about Pumpkin Jack, but we'll just call him Jack for now. He was a young boy at the time, full of energy and mischief, just like most other young boys that age, and treated his sister just like any other boys treated their sisters at that age.

But there was one thing different about Jack. He had something a lot of young boys and girls have at that age, a big imagination. He had a bigger amount of imagination than most other children, though.

It seemed to always interfere with what his parents were always asking him to do, to finish his homework or pick up his room or to stop picking on his sisters or to clean out the stables.

This was a job that Jack didn't particularly care for, but since cars were not allowed on the Island of the Land of Fall, people had to use horses and wagons to get to some places or to move stuff. There was a train, of course, but that only went over the stone and metal bridge to the mainland and it only went to the train house on the east side of town.

He didn't like to clean the stables, not because he didn't like to work, but because it took time away from his day dreaming. He did, however, like the horses that they owned, as he liked most of the horses in the town, so he didn't grumble too often or too much.

And his sister, Agatha (whom, of course, he called "Aggy") would often help him either with the stables or with his other chores, so he tried not to pick on her as often as he did his other sisters.

One morning before school, Jack was just daydreaming as usual while leaning on the pitchfork he used to clean the stalls. His thinking was interrupted by Agatha. She came into the stables, carrying both schoolbags for her and Jack in her hands and said,

"We need to get ready for school. What are you doing?"

Now, it was pretty obvious to Jack what he was doing, but he knew if he didn't speak up and say something, Agatha was likely to pinch him to see if he was asleep, as she often did at school.

"I'm thinking", he said.

"About what?" she replied.

"About how bored I am this morning."

She thought this over for a moment, and then asked,

"So, what are you going to do about it?"

"Do? Why, I'll... I'll... I'll start a parade, that's what I'll do!" His eyes lit up as the idea popped into his head and began to grow. A parade would be fun.

"A parade? What kind of parade?"

"Um, a... a dress-up parade! I'll wear Dad's volunteer fireman helmet and his gloves and boots and pretend to be a fireman leading the parade!"

"When would we have this parade?" asked Agatha.

"Today, after school" replied Jack as he put away the pitchfork and took his schoolbag from her.

"I want to be in the parade, too!" said Agatha.

"What are you going to dress up as?"

"Hmm", she said. "I'll have to think about that".

She walked out of the stables and Jack followed her out. He then went off down the road to the neighbor's house, where his best friend, Moley, lived. His name was really Maurice, but it was shortened to "Moley" by his friends.

"Moley!" Jack shouted as he came into their yard, and stood by the large walnut tree where they'd built a swing together the year before.

"Moley!"

"What?" The front door to their cottage opened and Moley stepped out. The first thing you noticed about Moley was his freckles. He had freckles on his face, freckles on his arms, and freckles on his legs. Jack often said he had freckles on his freckles. He was even sometimes called Freckled Moley by the other kids.

"What are you doing, Jack?"

"I want to start a parade after school today and I'd like you to help".

"Sure", said Moley, who had been just as bored that morning as Jack had been.

"What kind of parade?"

"A dress-up one. I'm going to wear my dad's fireman stuff. We'll get the other kids to do it, too, after school today."

"Oh, great" said Moley. "I can wear my uncle's tool belt and leather gloves he uses at his carpenter job. I'll let my mom know and I'll be right back."

Moley went back into his house and while Jack waited, he thought about all his friends, about Lyle, whose father worked as a bank teller on the mainland, about Samantha, whose mother was the village doctor, about Mary whose father was a dairy goat farmer and all the rest and how much they'd enjoy a parade, too.

After Moley came back out, they went to their friends' houses, who went to the other friends' houses, till every child in the village knew of the parade. Since that day was Friday, they thought it would be good to have it in the late afternoon, after school and suppers were over with.

That whole day as the news of the parade spread, the whole school was talking about it and how they were going to dress up. The history teacher, Mr. Gonfrey, even allowed them in the last period to make paper cutout masks with their parents' and families' faces drawn on them. That way the other kids could try to guess who they were supposed to be.

Each child went home and got all their items ready and put them aside for after supper, when they'd all join each other at the Fountain at dusk.

Now, normally, some people might think it kind of late for the children to be out at that time, but since it was in the town square by the fountain and it was very well lit by the street lamps there, everyone was able to come. Agatha was a little afraid of the dark, but she wasn't going to let that stop her from being in the parade. She had decided to come to the parade dressed as a princess. Her friend Mary decided that she would do something different and she would come as a pirate.

As the kids began to gather and then walk around the Fountain to show off their costumes and masks, the shop owners around the Fountain turned on their outside lights. Then Mrs. Bobson, the grocery store owner, came out to watch the kids march around in their costumes. She went back into the store, and came out with a large bowl of candy, and as each child walked by her, she handed them a piece of candy.

Soon, each kid had gone by her so many times that their hands were full of candy, so she handed each one of them a bag to hold their suckers and licorice twists and gumdrops and pieces of taffy and gum balls.

Not too long after the parade started, Mr. Ericksen, the vegetable farmer, came into the square with his wagon full of bushels of apples and other things for the grocery store, slowly and carefully edging his way between the marching children and the fountain. It was getting darker and he didn't want the horse to step on someone's foot.

As he pulled up by the fountain, a boy came around it with a cowboy hat and cap guns. The boy shot off one of the cap guns, startling the horse pulling the wagon, and the whole thing, horse, wagon, Mr. Ericksen and all, spilled into the pool of the fountain.

Mr. Ericksen went kersplash into the fountain and then stood up, snorting, soaking wet, his wiry black hair sticking out behind his ears, and an apple in his mouth.

Everyone who saw it started laughing and even Mr. Ericksen was laughing as he ate the apple. Then Moley got an idea. He walked up to the fountain, stuck his head in for a second and pulled it out with an apple in his mouth and his red hair sticking out in all directions, dripping wet. This also made everyone else laugh and soon they all had wet hair and apples in their mouths.

Then Jack got an idea. It was one of the most famous ideas in the history of the Land of Fall, even more famous than the Sawdust Wagon, and it came from Mrs. Bobson's street lamps.

You see, the other street lamps were square or boxy, but she liked roundish things, so she had two lamps in front of her store on low benches that were just large round balls with bulbs inside them.

Jack's idea was simple. One of the pumpkins had fallen from the cart and the bottom was busted open but the rest was fine. Jack picked it up, poked two holes for eyes in the pumpkin and put it over one of the lamps in front of Mrs. Bobson's grocery store.

The bulb's light shone from the eyes and everyone thought it was a fine idea. Soon, they were taking the other broken pumpkins and poking holes in them, too, to see what kind of shapes they could make.

Everyone had a great time at the parade, and the school, in fact, the whole town, was talking about the parade for a long time afterward.

Because of Jack's poking holes in the pumpkin, he got the nickname "Pumpkin Jack". As he grew up, and gained in popularity and wisdom, when it came time for the town to pick a new mayor, they all decided Jack would be the best person for the job.

Eventually, his long nickname was shortened to "Mayor Jack" and each mayor after him would hold him up as an example of how to rule the town. Soon, people just started calling the mayor "Mayor Jack", regardless of who he or she was.

People liked Jack and the Parade near the Fountain so much, they decided to hold the parade every year, at about the same time, even with the apple bobbing. But they decided to do it in buckets instead of the Fountain because it was easier for more people to do it and that way only your head got wet.

They also continued the passing out of candy, though the townspeople bought it from Mrs. Bobson, and the dressing up. They decided to call it "the Parade of the

Fountain", and eventually it was shortened to just "the Parade".

And that's the story of how Pumpkin Jack and the Fountain came to be. There are other stories, too, like Uncle Robert's Fish Stew and A Giant's Belt, but the next story is about The Sawdust Wagon.

The Sawdust Wagon

So, another story from the Green Man. I'd met him many times before in the coffee shop that I hang out in when I try to write. I was in there one bright fall day, taking a writing break for a moment and having a coffee and a bagel when he came in.

He was called the Green Man. Not a Blue Man or an Orange Man or even a Purple Man but a Green Man. And, of course, not because of green hair or green eyes but because of what he always wore. He wore a green shirt, green pants, green shoes, and a floppy fade green hat that, like all his clothes, looked as if it had seen better days.

This was a fall day that was typical of a lot of fall days around the coffee shop. There was just a hint of wood smoke smell from somewhere. The leaves were still on the trees though some of them had fallen and were eager to scramble around on the sidewalk under your feet as you passed. There was a nip in the air but mostly in the evenings and it wasn't unpleasant to wear a sweater or heavier jacket and slowly stroll around, looking at the stars that way.

He came through the double doors of the shop, making the door's bell tinkle, then after seeing me, slid into his usual spot at the booth across from me. He ordered his usual green tea from the waitress, paused a moment and then spoke.

"What are you doing?"

Now, he always found me here writing, but I knew that he meant to ask what I was writing about. I wasn't writing on my yellow pads like I normally did but in a lined notebook.

"I'm writing a letter to a friend of mine overseas, someone I've never met" I said as I continued writing.

"Oh, a pen pal?"

"Yes, that's what they used to call them" I said.

"Anima did that once. She wrote to her family about The Sawdust Wagon."

"Anima, Mary's friend from the Land of Fall? And what in the world is a Sawdust Wagon?"

"Yes, she was writing to some relatives in another country about her friends she'd made on the Island."

He launched into his tale about Anima and the Wagon and the normally cheery coffee shop seemed even cheerier for his telling of it.

We've discussed the Land of Fall before, you and I. We've talked about how it's always fall there, how the trees look beautiful in their colors and the burning bushes seem particularly bright and how the season rarely changes.

Some things do change on the Island, though. It's just rarer than at other places. One of those such changes was when Anima and her family came to the Island.

The school on the Island was located in Scarecrow Corners, the biggest of the three villages. The school was an old brick building, with four-paned wooden windows and steam radiators for heat on the chillier days. Some kids said it was the oldest building on the Island. It had four classrooms, one for each set of grades, separated into the youngest, elementary, middle school and high school grades.

There was a central hallway that ran between them, two to a side, back to the offices for the school. The classrooms were close enough that if the students were just a bit louder than normal, they could be heard in the other three rooms. Since the school was so small, all the kids knew each other and their parents. The same students each year helped with the Fountain Parade and the Thanksgiving celebration and the roles in the Thanksgiving play generally went to the same students.

Then Anima and her parents moved to the Island. The first news of this was brought to the school by Freckled Moley, who had heard it from his mom.

"Jack, guess what?" he asked his friend one day as they sat down to eat their lunches in the small cafeteria room at the end of the long office hallway.

"I don't know" said Jack, through a mouthful of hot dog and bun and relish.   "What?"

"There's a new kid coming to the Island."

"What? A new kid? How do you know?" asked Agatha, Jack's older sister, as she sat down next to Moley with her lunch plate. "What's he look like?"

"I don't know what she looks like but my mom said she might look a little different" said Moley as he picked up his sandwich and began to eat.

"Oh?" said Agatha. "Different clothes? Ten feet tall? Three arms?"

Moley laughed and said,

"No. I don't know how. But my mom asked me if I'd go over to the old Fredericks farm after school today. They're moving into that place and they're going to be our neighbors. She wanted me to take them a pie or something to welcome them."

"Can I come along?" asked Agatha.

"Sure" said Moley. "It might be nice for her to have another girl to talk to."

41

The new kid was the buzz of the school for the rest of the day and even The Mary That Wouldn't decided, this time, that she would, in fact, go with them and see the new girl.

After school, there were only three kids that could come along with Moley and they brought presents they'd gotten from their desks. Mary kept an extra red and silver hair ribbon there, Moley had a notebook that he hadn't used yet for school and Agatha had a collapsible cup she'd gotten as a present from her mother that she kept in her desk, intending to use it at school but never did. They all went to Moley's house along with him so he could get the pie. His mother was famous on the Island for her strawberry-rhubarb pie and they all thought it was a good thing to give a new family just coming to the Island.

"Wait. If we're going to bring them a pie and these presents, what about bringing MissV also?" said Agatha as they left the schoolhouse.

MissV was the floppy-eared, brushy-tailed canine guardian of the old bookstore that Mr. Boot ran. She wasn't thought to be much of a guardian, since she was older and moved a little slow to be any sort of effective guardian. But she was great at greeting customers as they came into the shop and the kids thought this would be a good thing to bring to the new family.

"Well, if we're going to be bringing them a pie and presents and a visit from MissV, I think we should all bring something as well, including you, Jack" said Mary. Moley, Agatha and Jack stopped and thought.

"I could bring her.. I could bring her... what can I bring her, Aggy?" asked Jack to his sister.

Agatha thought for a moment. Moley thought for a moment. Mary thought for a moment. Finally, Jack got an idea.

"I know" he said. "I could bring her one of the shells from my collection from the beach."

"That's a good idea but I have maybe a better one, Jack" suggested Agatha. "How about we stop at the beach along the way and look for a new shell for her?"   They all thought this was a good idea so they walked to the beach, never far away on the Island, and began looking for shells. Jack found a couple of good crab shells and Agatha found some neat snail shells and Moley found some pretty clam shells and Mary even found a small conch shell. They didn't know what to carry all the stuff in until Moley said,

"I have an old wagon at my house that I was going to throw out after my mom bought me a new one. Let's go there and put the stuff in that."

So they took the shells and the book and the ribbon and the notebook and they all walked to Moley's house.

When they got there, Moley went to the small shed and got out the old wagon. It was made mostly of wood painted brown, with big flat-sided wooden wheels, a wood bed and wooden slats around the sides. The only metal parts were the axles and the handle, which were a rusty red color.

"What if the shells break on the way there?" asked Mary, worriedly.

"Hmm" said Jack.

"Hmm" said Moley.

"Hmm" said Agatha. Then, "Wait, I know! Let's put sawdust from the pile at the back of the shed into the wagon to make a soft bed for the shells."

So they got a bucket from the shed and filled it and dumped it into the wagon, then repeated that a few more times till it was half full of sawdust. They smoothed it out with their hands and laid the presents on top of the sawdust. To keep the ribbon clear of the sawdust, Mary tied it around the wagon handle.

They all thought that looked grand enough to carry the presents so they started back along the road to the bookstore to get MissV to travel with them to the Fredericks farm. Agatha and Mary and Jack and Moley all took turns pulling the wagon.

They stopped at the bookstore and asked Mr. Boot if MissV could travel with them. As she had gone on many walks with the children before and she was known to be not only a Good

Judge of Character but also a Good Friend, he was delighted to let her go along with them when he found out the purpose of the children's' trip.

They had just left the bookstore with MissV in tow when Agatha said,

"I hope she likes these presents. I wonder what her name is?"

They spent the rest of the walk to the Ericksen's farm trying to come up with names for the new girl and her family.

The farmhouse was nestled in a small grove just over the hill from Moley's house. As they topped the hill, Mary pointed and said,

"Look! They're out in the yard."

The four children stood there for a moment, watching the new family.

The first thing they noticed was what was apparently the girl's father. He was a stout man and apparently very strong. He was lifting up big boxes

from Mr. Ericksen's wagon by himself
and carrying them into the house. He
had dark brown hair and a mustache
almost as long as Mr. Grimbleson's.
There was a young boy, maybe two or
three years old, playing with the
flowers that grew along the side of the
fence in the front of the yard. He was
very chubby and looked like he was
giggling a lot.

There were two boys a bit older that
were obviously twins; if they stood
facing each other, it looked like a living
mirror. Then there was the mother and
the girl. Both wore long dresses, very
prettily patterned, the mother's dress
decorated in blue patterns, the
daughter's dress done in green. They
each also wore head scarves of bright
colorful patterns that matched their
dresses.

Mr. Ericksen came out of the house,
walking toward the wagon. He looked

up the hill, saw the children and waved them down.

As they came into the yard, Jack now pulling the wagon, MissV next to him, the two girls and then Moley bringing up the rear, they all suddenly felt shy. What if the new girl didn't like the presents?

Mr. Ericksen realized the children's dilemma and decided to help.

"MissV!" he called and the dog trotted quickly (for her) to him, stopping right in front of him and the youngest boy as the farmer began to talk to her and pet her.

The baby giggled and laughed at the big dog, who promptly kissed him many times on the face, making him laugh even more. As the kids came up, Mr. Ericksen said,

"Children, this is a new family on the Island." He motioned to the father and then around to the rest of the family in turn. "This is Ahsan, this is his wife, Enakshi, these are the twins, Raji and Haji, this is the baby, Naarad and this is their daughter, Anima."

He looked at the wagon and smiled.

"And what is it you have there?"

"It's a present for Anima" said Mary, after a moment, for the others seemed tongue-tied. "We wanted to welcome her to the school. This is a bunch of shells and a notebook and a pie Moley's mother baked and a cup and a-"

She was interrupted by Anima.

"Oh, they've brought me a wagon, I've never had one!" She smiled very broadly and took the handle from Jack's unresisting hand as they took the rest of the presents off the wagon. Her twin brothers immediately climbed into the wagon and began telling her,

"Pull us, pull us!"

So she pulled them round and round the front of the yard and the boys laughed and the baby laughed and everyone, yes, even Mary, laughed.

"Moley" said Mr. Ericksen, still smiling. "That was a nice thing that all of you did. Bringing all those presents and even a wagon for the new girl."

Moley looked at Mr. Ericksen and knew that the farmer knew the wagon wasn't originally meant as a prize. If he said something about it, he knew Mr. Ericksen would find a way to get his wagon back. But the boys were having such fun with it.

"Yes, Mr. Ericksen. They should have lots of fun with it" said Moley, smiling, as he watched Anima and her brothers play with the wagon.

Then they all took turns playing with the wagon and being pulled by the other kids or Mr. Ericksen or Anima's father until everyone had sawdust in their hair and their clothes and giggles were still coming out. They all shared in a small piece of the pie baked by Moley's mom and it was generally agreed that it was a wonderful pie.

The children all waved to Anima and her family as they rode away on the back of Mr. Ericksen's wagon.

"We'll see you tomorrow at school!" called Mary.

"I'll be there" said Anima. "And thanks again for the presents!"

The next morning at school, the children told all their friends about the new girl. When she came into the classroom with Mr. Grimbleson, she looked a little timid but, upon seeing the smiles of Mary and Agatha and Jack and Moley, smiled back and looked like she felt better.

"Class, we have a new girl today and her name is-

" Mr. Grimbleson was interrupted by the whole class saying,

"Anima!"

He smiled and they all laughed and he showed Anima which desk she would use. As she put her books on it, he went to the chalkboard behind his desk and pulled down the world atlas map he used for geography lessons.

"Anima, can you come and show the class where the rest of your family is from?"

Anima walked up to the map, looked at it for a moment then pointed to a small town far across the map from the Island.

"Thank you, Anima" said Mr. Grimbleson. "You may sit down. Now, class " he said, as Anima took her seat, "That's a long distance away. I have an idea. Why don't we write a letter to Anima's family that lives there? We can tell them about the Island and about the presents you gave her yesterday and about how much fun she can have here."

The class thought that was a great idea. They passed around a notebook page and each child got to write one sentence to Anima's family about the Island. Then Mr. Grimbleson wrote about the presents and how glad they were that Anima and her family had come to the Island to live. Then he got another piece of paper, had every child sign it, put both pieces into a large envelope and put a stamp on it.

"Can you come up and write the address on the envelope, Anima? Then I think we can take a short field trip to the post office to mail it."

Anima came up and very carefully wrote her family's address on the envelope. Then Mr. Grimbleson wrote the school's address and "From

Anima's Class" on the top corner of the envelope. They all left the classroom, grabbed their coats from the coat room and headed outside.

Once they were all outside and ready, Mr. Grimbleson led the way to the post office. This was actually, though Anima didn't know it, the bookstore that Mr. Boot ran as well.

When they came into the bookstore, MissV woofed slightly once and got up to walk over to Anima, wagging her tail. She licked Anima's hand, then went to lay back down by the stove.

"She apparently likes you, young lady" said Mr. Boot from behind his counter, Turner Jake nodding in agreement from his stool beside the stove. "She is a good judge of character and that is enough for me. How may I be of assistance to you?"

"We would like to mail a letter to this student's family" said Mr. Grimbleson, nodding once at Anima and then handing the envelope to Mr. Boot.

"Oh, my" he said, approvingly. "That's quite a ways. I think you have the distinction, young lady, of being the person who has mailed a letter the longest distance so far from this post office."

Anima blushed slightly and nodded.

"Thank you, sir" she said.

"No, I must thank you and ask you a favor. If you would be so kind as to ask your family to write something, anything in return, I would be most gratified to know that I had assisted in such a long distance communication."

Anima looked puzzled till Mary whispered to her,

"He means he's glad to send a letter back and forth for so long."

"Ahh" said Anima. "Thank you again, then, sir".

So, after they mailed the letter, the class went back to the classroom where the geography lesson didn't seem quite so boring that day. Anima had made some new friends and the children were happy for her and themselves.

That is how the story of The Sawdust Wagon came to be and how it became a tradition of sorts, when they moved onto the Island, to take a new family some housewarming gifts in a wagon full of sawdust. The next tale is a bit different, since it focuses on The Mary That Wouldn't and how even though she deserved her name, she wasn't like that all the time.

Uncle Robert's
Fish Stew

I've told you in the previous stories about the Green Man, about why he's called the Green Man (because all he wears is green), about how he visits me sometimes in the local coffee shop and about his stories, the wonderful stories.

Sometimes he shows up in the summer, sometimes in the winter. Sometimes he comes when it's pouring rain and the cafe windows are fogged up. I never know when he's going to be there.

One day I was puzzling over a story and my frustration must have made me think hard about the story and not much else because I wasn't aware anyone else was in the cafe that morning until I heard a soft "ahem" and looked up and there he was.

All in green, of course. This time, since it was raining pretty steadily outside and had been for most of the week, he wore his usual green shirt, green shoes, green pants and green (and now very wet) old floppy leather hat. It was all covered by a faded green raincoat, torn a little on the edges and obviously having seen better days.

He sat down in the seat across the booth from me and ordered his usual green tea when the waitress came by.

"What are you working on" he asked softly, his voice sort of somehow rhyming with the rain drumming on the cafe's windows.

"This story is difficult" I said. "I've been working on it very hard but don't seem to be getting anywhere. I might just give up on it."

"No, don't do that. Do what Mary did."

"Mary?" I asked, knowing where it was leading.

"Yes" he replied "The Mary That Wouldn't."

"That Wouldn't What?"

"Ahh, that was the question, wasn't it? And her uncle was involved, as you know how uncles can sometimes be. And if it weren't for the help of her friends..."

As he warmed up to telling the tale, I forgot my story, I forgot my coffee and I forgot the rain. I just sat and listened. And even though it was about the Land of Fall, it was still, somehow, about me...

So, as I said, once upon a time, the seasons didn't change much in the

Land of Fall. Oh, yes, the flowers would bloom for a week or so, the hot days would come with ice cream and cotton candy, and the kids would slide down the hill on the snow behind the schoolhouse in Scarecrow Corners.

But those only lasted a week or so, each one, and the season of fall in the Land of Fall went on for months; the chilled mornings, frost barely showing on the sides of the windowpanes; the dry, colorful leaves that covered the sidewalks and dusty lanes between the villages; the smell of wood fires filling the air. This particular story takes during the middle of the fall season.

There were and are many people living in the Land of Fall. They do live in all three villages. One of the best known is Uncle Robert and one of the things he's best known for is his fish stew.

One of the more pleasant places to warm up was at Uncle Robert's house and he was one of the more popular people on the Island.

He wasn't everyone's uncle but everyone called him that because he seemed like their uncle and Robert was a Friendly Sort of Uncle.
You know the kind; funny, warmhearted, wise, soothing, the kind of uncle who was willing to have many many nieces and nephews, even if they didn't exactly have the same last name as he did.

One of his nieces who did have the same last name was Mary. And Mary wasn't as pleasant as her uncle was. Mary wasn't just called Mary, although she was to her face.

Mary didn't like to do much of anything that she hadn't thought of, or seemed fun, or was interesting and so Mary got the reputation of being, well, sort of, of being kind of stubborn. And since she especially didn't like doing anything that anyone else asked her to do, she soon got the nickname of The Mary That Wouldn't.

Wouldn't what, you ask? Well, most anything.

It was one fine day in mid fall, when the leaves were just starting to come down and people all around the island were getting ready for the harvests and piling things in sheds and checking weather forecasts and muttering about not having enough storage space and where am I going to put all that zucchini while we still have some from last year's crop and- well, you get the idea. They were busy. But not Mary. Oh, no, not her.

It was Saturday morning so she had no school and the only thing she was doing, she was doing now, and that was walking to her Uncle Robert's house.

The reason she was walking there is that her Uncle Robert always made her favorite meal, fish stew, for supper on the second Saturday of the month, which this was. For some strange reason that Mary could never quite figure out, her Uncle Robert wouldn't bring the soup to Mary's house which seemed to Mary to be the reasonable thing to do. Oh, no, Mary had to walk to his house.

But this massive effort, this huge sacrifice on Mary's part (as Mary thought it to be) was worth it, as far as she was concerned. Because nobody could cook as well as her Uncle Robert. Oh, her mother was a fair cook and did grand pies and nice pastries and tolerable stews and all those sorts of things but nothing like Uncle Robert's pies and pastries and stews.

And his fish stew was the best. It had the best fish in it and the best onions and the best potatoes and the best everything and Mary loved it.

Mary walked up to her Uncle Robert's house, a trim stone cottage set against the edge of the only forest on the Island and knocked, then swung open the door to the hallway. She scraped the mud off her boots as her Uncle Robert came out of the kitchen.

"Why, what are you doing here, Mary?" asked Uncle Robert with a twinkle in his eye.

"Uncle Robert " said Mary, shaking her finger at him and pretending to be cross, "you know it's the second Saturday of the month and you know you always make your fish stew on that day."

"Why, yes, I do" he said, a little sadly. "But I have a problem this time, Mary. I don't know if I can make the stew this week."

Mary's heart sank at the thought of not having that wonderful stew.

"Why not?"

"Well, child, I'm making a surprise birthday cake for Mrs. Bobson, the store owner. It's in the oven now and I can't leave it till it's done. And I made so much fish stew last time that I ran out of things and I need a bunch of things for it this time."

Mary thought for a moment then offered what was, for her, a very good deed, in her eyes.

"I can go get those things for you, Uncle Robert" she said. "I'll do just about anything for your fish stew."

"Are you sure? You're going to have to get everything on the list and carry it all back by yourself. I can't go with you."

Hearing that that much work was involved, Mary had second thoughts for a moment, but it was her Uncle Robert's fish stew, after all.

"Yes, I'm sure."

"Okay, Mary. Here's the list of things I need and here's a burlap bag to carry it all in. Don't forget, if I don't get everything on that list, I can't make the soup."

Mary nodded, took the bag and the list and stuck them in her pockets then went back to the hallway and put her boots on. As she walked outside, she pulled the list back out of her pocket and looked at it.

As she opened it and started to read, she almost dropped it. 'Look at all the things on this list!' she thought. 'It will take me forever to get

everything. How am I supposed to get
them all in time?'

But the memory of that
wonderful stew made her determined
to get everything on the list, even if she
had to... she had to... well, you know...
she had to work for it.

The first thing on the list was
the dried fish that was the main
ingredient for the soup and so Mary set
off down the lane to the dock near the
train station house, which was where
the fish seller had his shop.

As she walked up to it, she
thought, not for the first time, what an
odd looking shop it was, too.

It was all made of rough oak
planks and beams and pieces of tin
nailed here and there to stop leaks,
though it didn't look like that worked
too well. As she got close, she could
smell the fish smell and the smoke
coming out of the back area of the shop

where the fish seller kept his stove for drying the fish he sold.

The fish seller, a short, wide, grizzled old man named Barney Almond, came out to pile some packages of fish on the counter and saw her. He smiled at her and said,

"Let me guess, Mary. You wouldn't be wanting any of my dried cod for your uncle's stew now, would you?"

"Yessir, Mr. Nut, I would."

The fish seller's last name was Almond but he asked everyone to call him Mr. Nut which he got a chuckle out of, every time.

"Hmm. I only have enough for one package and I know Samantha's mother, Dr. Durham, will be wanting a package tomorrow for her regular fish and chips. I tell you what, if you help me salt up a package for her so I can put it in the smoker to be ready by tomorrow, then you can have this one for your uncle's stew, okay?"

This was a little more than Mary had bargained for but after all, it was her uncle Robert's fish stew and she also couldn't deny Dr. Durham her fish fry either, could she? So she grimaced and set her basket on the counter and went in to help Mr. Almond salt the fish.

It wasn't actually that hard of work to do, just a lot of messing with oily fish and scales and big chunks of salt crystals and whew, did her hands stink when she was done! But Mr. Almond had a sink right there and some good peach-smelling soap to wash her hands with and soon she was all cleaned up.

So she took the package of dried fish, put it in the burlap bag and waved to Mr. Almond and went out the door, heading for Mr. Fitzgerald's farm across the east side of the dock.

As she walked up the driveway to the small house, Mr. Fitzgerald came out of the small barn next to it. He had a dark blue stocking cap covering his otherwise well-weathered head and a pitchfork and shovel in his sun-browned hands.

"What can I do for you, Mary?" he asked as he leaned on the shovel handle.

"Well, Mr. Fitzgerald, you know it's the second Saturday of the month and you know my uncle Robert always makes fish stew on this day. But he's run out of ingredients so she gave me a list of what to get and who to get it from and from you, she wants to know if she can get-" here, she paused and pulled the list from her pocket to look at it.

"Onions, Mr. Fitzgerald. Onions."

"Well, Mary, I do have onions, that's a fact. But I have a problem."

"What's that?" Mary's heart sank.

"Well, I had a storage bin in the barn that had shelves in it where I kept my onions and apples and rutabagas and turnips and things. But it was made of old wood and not very sturdy and those pesky rats chewed through the leather straps I had holding it up trying to get to all those things.

So the whole thing fell down and I have apples and onions and turnips all over the floor of the barn. It'll take me a long time to sort it out... unless, that is, you want to help."

'Well' thought Mary 'at least it's not cold slimy fish'.

So she agreed to help Mr. Fitzgerald. She put her burlap bag by the side of the open door of the barn and he put aside the shovel and pitchfork.

They went in and started sorting through the pile on the floor, making other piles separately. Soon it was done and Mr. Fitzgerald handed her two of the biggest yellowest onions he had and she put them in her burlap bag and went down the lane to the next person.

Now this next person, Mary wasn't so comfortable visiting. It was the house of Mr. Grimbleson, one of the teachers at the school. He was nice and everything but he made Mary do homework which, as you know, has the word work in it and therefore was something Mary really didn't want to do. But she did do it, mostly to keep both Mr. Grimbleson and her parents from complaining to her about it too often.

His cottage was made of mostly stone with a wood-tiled roof and really looked rather neat, if you didn't mind the occupant. She went up and knocked on the door and stepped back as Mr. Grimbleson opened it.

He was a fairly lean man, clean-shaven but for the longest mustache she'd ever seen on anyone. He even shaved his head or at least, it looked like it, all shiny and smooth.

"What can I do for you, Mary?"

"Well, Mr. Grimbleson, it's Saturday and my uncle Robert wants-"

"Wants to make fish stew, I presume?"

"Yes, sir. I've been gathering ingredients."

"Does he need something else?"

"Yes, sir." Mary looked at the list again. "He needs potatoes, at least three or four big ones."

"Hmm" said Mr. Grimbleson. "I don't have any big ones in the pantry. But I was just going out to see if there were any new ones I could dig up yet. Why don't you come and help me and that way you can have first choice of what you want?"

Mary sighed (inwardly, of course). More work. But she knew she wanted the stew so she waited till Mr. Grimbleson got his coat on and came outside and grabbed a shovel and a bucket from his small shed. Then they walked around to the back of the cottage where Mr. Grimbleson's garden lay.

She could see the rows of carrots, radishes and corn to one side and the area where he'd planted the potatoes.

"Here, Mary" he said as he handed her the bucket. "You hold the bucket and I'll dig. Then, when we're done with two rows, we'll go in and sort the potatoes."

So Mary held the bucket as Mr. Grimbleson dug. At first, it was easy because the bucket was empty. But as he went along the row, the bucket got heavier and heavier. At the end of the first row, it was so heavy that she had a hard time carrying it. He noticed that she was struggling with it and said,

"Okay, Mary. I think that's enough for this row. Let's go in and sort them out and see if there's any in there that might be good enough for your uncle's stew."

So they went in to the cottage, into the kitchen area and Mr.

Grimbleson dumped all the potatoes into the sink and they filled it with water, then scrubbed off the potatoes.

There were four large ones, just ripened and not green, that both she and Mr. Grimbleson thought would be good for the soup. So she took them and put them into the burlap bag. She said her thank yous and her goodbyes to Mr. Grimbleson, pretending not to hear his admonition to her about her homework being done for the next week and set off down the lane for the next person on the list.

'Finally', she thought as she took the list out of her pocket and looked at it once more. 'Only one more thing to go'. And that thing was cream. She could have gotten it first, being as the only dairy farm on the island wasn't too far from her uncle Robert's house.

But she would have had to go back to her uncle Robert's house right away so that he could put the cream in the refrigerator so it wouldn't go bad. And then back out again to get the stuff she'd already gotten. No, it was much better this way. Less walking and less work.

She walked alongside the wooden fence leading to the Danner's cow pasture. As she walked along she saw movement behind the curtains of the house near the pasture, then the door opened and Willy Danner came out.

Willy was the Danner's only boy out of five children and having four sisters did not normally make him like girls too much. But he and Mary sat next to each other at school and he was a smart kid and sometimes helped Mary with her homework, in part because Mary didn't tease him like any of his sisters often did.

"Hi, Mary. What are you doing?"

"I'm collecting stuff to help my uncle Robert make his fish stew."

"Oh, good. I had that once, it was really good."

"Do you have any cream?"

"Well, we do and we don't. We have some but not very much. But I was about to go out and skim the cream out of the tubs. If you want, you can come and help and then get plenty of cream."

"Sure, I'll help. I can't go back without it."

So Mary walked in with Willy to the side of the barn where the milk tubs sat. They were special warming tubs and had ladles hung on the side of them. Willy went to a shelf and pulled out a cardboard box of large jars and sat it on a stool next to the tubs.

He took a ladle and showed Mary how to slowly skim off the cream so that it was thick and not runny from too much milk, then to ladle it into the jars.

Soon they had all the jars full and Willy put lids on them. Then he grabbed another burlap bag, filled it with straw and put two of the jars carefully inside it.

"Here you go" he said as he handed it to her. "This will be plenty for your uncle's stew today and the next time."

"Thanks, Willy. That's the last ingredient I need, finally, I'm done! I can go back to my uncle's house now."

Mary picked up both bags, being a little more careful with the one with the jars of cream in it and set off down the road, finally heading back toward her uncle's house.

Her feet and legs were tired from the walking, her arms were tired from the digging and the carrying, and she just wanted to get back to her uncle's house.

Finally, she walked up the steps to the front door and rapped at the door with her foot, since her hands were full.

Her uncle opened the door and took the burlap bags from Mary, carrying them into the house as Mary followed him down the hallway into the kitchen.

"Sit there in the chair, Mary. So, did you get everything?"

"Yes, sir" Mary yawned as she sat down and laid her head on her arms on the table. "I had to help Mr. Almond salt the fish and then I had to help Mr. Fitzgerald sort his onions and then I had to help Mr. Grimbleson dig his potatoes and then I had to help Willy skim the cream and carry it all back here. I think I walked around the world!"

"Well, not quite" Uncle Robert said as he laughed and took the things out of the bags and put the cream and everything else on the counter next to the stove.

He opened a drawer and got out a large knife and his old hickory cutting board and began cutting up the vegetables.

"But you know what you did do, Mary?"

He didn't wait for her to answer but went on.

"You worked for it! You got the fish, you got the onions, you got the potatoes, you got the cream. And you did the carrying and getting all by yourself! What do you think about that?"

Hearing no answer, Uncle Robert turned from his vegetable cutting board to see Mary with her head laying on her arm, eyes closed, sleeping at the table.

'Hmpf' said Uncle Robert to himself as he turned back to his vegetables. 'She'll wake up in time for supper, she won't miss that if I know that girl'.

So The Mary That Wouldn't figured prominently in that story and she did very well for herself and her family and friends. The next story also involves that same Mary but she doesn't fare quite as well...

A Turkey In A Basket

The Green Man Tells A Turkey Of A Tale

Once upon a time... no, really, it did start out that way, the story did, and I'm not one to change some part of a story just because it's not the most Modern Thing, or because a lot of other stories start differently than that.

Now, this story was told to me on a cold winter's day with the snow blowing and the wind whistling through your ears like ... well, like the wind would whistle if it whistled through your ears. And I was hunkered down in the coffee shop with my pads and pens and worn leather briefcase making a sort of second desk on the booth's tabletop when who should walk in but the Green Man again.

We won't go over again in great detail as to why he's called The Green Man because we've already covered that little bit of the story. We've already discussed his green clothes and his green floppy leather hat. Just where he bought an old green parka, I don't know.

But we'll just note something that happened, that day, even with the snowdrifts around the lamp poles on the sidewalk outside the cafe, even with the other patrons visibly shivering every time someone opened the double doors into the main part of the cafe and let the fingers of that sharp north wind slide in between coat sleeves and alongside knees only covered in panty hose.

Just the entering into the coffee shop by the Green Man seemed to brighten up the place a bit, even now in the deep days of winter. People talked a little bit more freely, their eyes seemed more awake and looking round the room as if to say, huh, even though it's cold outside, it's toasty warm in here.

He spied me at my usual corner booth and walked over and sat down, nodding to the waitress who, knowing his habits didn't change, brought him a large cup of green tea.

"Little chilly outside to be wearing just that thin parka, isn't it?" I asked as he slid into the booth across from me.

"Not too bad. But then, you know I like a bit of nip in the air. How are you doing?"

"Oh, I'm doing fine. I'm trying to write up a poster for the Thanksgiving parade that's coming."

"Ahhh, Thanksgiving. Did I ever tell you about the time when there almost wasn't a Thanksgiving because of a certain person on the Island of the Land of Fall and the Turkeys That Had Gone Missing?"

"No, you haven't."

As he began to warm up to his tale, I got lost in the telling of it and forgot about the snow and the traffic and even the poster I was working on.

You see, there was this turkey that... Wait, that's not right. Let me start again, with the beginning of the story.

This story starts with the Mary Who Wouldn't, although she got that name for reasons besides just what happened in this story. But this Mary had a Secret. And it wasn't the Kind Of Secret that might have gotten her into trouble, or the kind of secret that might have gotten anyone else into trouble.

It wasn't very much of a Secret, to be frank, in anyone's eyes but Mary. Because she didn't know that most other people knew it and it had to do, in large part, with how The Mary That Wouldn't got her name.

Mary didn't like meat. Now, not just big plump hot dogs in a bun, not even with relish and mustard or spicy hamburgers, not even with pickles and cheese, or savory pork chops or tender roasts of beef or steaming mutton pies or tangy barbecued chicken or... where was I? Oh, yes, sorry, this was about Mary.

Yes, she didn't like any kind of meat. It didn't matter what it was in, or how it was made or who cooked it. She didn't like it. Why she didn't like it, no one knows, although Mary's friend, Jack (yes, that Jack) thought perhaps that it was just because she was The Mary Who Wouldn't. But he kept those thoughts to himself, especially around Mary.

So Mary's family helped keep up the pretense for her. Her mother, a good cook in any situation, would make extra servings of beans or mashed potatoes or the occasional eggplant Parmesan. Her brothers and her parents would pass the plate with meat on it to Mary just in case she changed her mind but she always seemed to be full and said no, thank you.

But there was a holiday coming up on which Mary always found it hard to say no thank you. Every time Thanksgiving rolled around, some of Mary's cousins came across the water on the train from the mainland. And they were meat eaters, whoo, boy, let me tell you! Every time they came, they talked about smoked sausages and cured hams and roasted ducks and necks in gravy and turkey wings and other bits of meat till Mary would think of some reason to go to her bedroom, perhaps to find something, and not come out till they'd gone.

But on Thanksgiving, she couldn't do that because they usually stayed the weekend and went back on Sunday evenings. And that was a long time, even for Mary, to be looking for something in her bedroom.

Last year, she noticed they'd been making comments about how there seemed to be a lot of food left and was Mary sure she was full? They'd ask her if perhaps a turkey wing or helping of sausage stuffing might tide her over, just for the day?

One of the things Mary disliked above all else was being made to do something she didn't really want to do and she thought long and hard in the days before Thanksgiving to try and come up with a plan. She thought and thought and thought until she couldn't think any more about it. Then, one day at school, it came to her.

'If there's no turkey" she thought "then there'll be no relatives trying to make me eat it!'

But how would she get rid of the turkey? Her father bought one every year from Mr. Ericksen who had the largest farm on the island (especially since it was the only real farm on the island). He fattened up a handful of turkeys for sale every year and they all sold fairly quickly.

She had to either stop her father from buying the turkey, not a likely thing considering how much the rest of her family liked turkey, or somehow make the turkeys disappear.

'Aha!' she thought excitedly. 'That's it, I'll make the turkeys disappear! But... how?' Then she got the Idea, the Idea that would be remembered on the Island for a long time afterward. 'But I'll need help.'

She looked around the classroom at the other students and one by one, decided they were too short or too slow or too timid or too... Not Right For The Job. And at last, finally, she came to the student, the one student that she knew she could count on. She decided to ask one of her best friends who had never let her down before. Anny.

Now, Anny wasn't her real name. Anima was her real name. When she first arrived on the island, Mary hadn't talked to her much because Anima was shy around people she didn't know all that well and Mary was, too, though she'd never admit it. Since Anima dressed a little differently than other kids on the island did, she was a little bit shy with new people.

But one day, at lunch, Mary noticed that Anima didn't take the chicken they were offering that day. She didn't think anything much of it till the next day when Anima didn't take the hot dogs and the day after that when Anima didn't take the spare ribs. So Mary watched her for a few more days and Anima never took any of the meat.

Finally, Mary came over one day at lunchtime to the table where Anima was sitting and sat down.

"Can I ask you something, Anima?" said Mary as she sat down across the table from her.

"Sure" said Anima.

"I noticed you don't take any meat" said Mary quietly, so the other kids couldn't hear. "Why is that?"

"No one in my family eats meat" said Anima. "And I've never eaten it."

Mary sighed sort of sadly. "I wish my family was like that. I don't like meat and... and I keep having to pretend I do."

Anima thought for a moment, then said,

"Why not come over to our house once in a while? I'm sure my mother won't mind and you won't have to worry about eating meat over there."

From that point on, Mary and Anima were good friends. Mary would often ask her mother if she could go over to Anny's house for supper and it was always okay, although her mother did wonder in the beginning why Anny never seemed to want to come to their house for supper.

"Pssst, Anny" said Mary in a whisper as she handed a note to Jimmy, the boy who sat in front of her, to give to Anny. "Read this and talk to me at lunchtime, okay?" Anny took the paper from Jimmy, read it and nodded.

Later, in the cafeteria, the two girls sat at their usual table and thought up their plan.

"This coming Thursday is Thanksgiving again. We need to make the turkeys disappear" said Mary in a voice low enough that the other children couldn't hear her.

"Yes, but how?" asked Anny.

"We can open the gate in the fence and they'll just wander out. By the time anyone notices, it will be too late to catch them for Thanksgiving dinner."

"Only if we do it that morning" said Anny.

"Otherwise, they'll just catch them and it won't do any good."

"Okay. So we need to come up with a reason to get away. How about if I ask my mother if I can ask your mother if you can come to my house for Thanksgiving dinner? And you ask your mother the same thing?"

"That's a great idea, Mary. We'll both be gone and our parents will think we're at each other's house!"

They finished their lunches quickly and went back to class, happy and sort of excited thinking about the results when their plan was put to work.

That following Saturday, Mary got up early in the morning like she did every Thanksgiving morning to help her mother with the baking and cooking. But this morning, though her mother didn't know it, was something special.

"Mom, can I ask a favor?" said Mary as she got out the eggs and butter from the refrigerator to set on the table where her mother was measuring spices and flour into her cookie-mixing bowl.

"Sure, Mary. What's the favor?"

"Well, I'd like to go ask Anny's mom if Anny can come to our house for Thanksgiving dinner. If that's alright."

Her mother looked oddly at Mary for a moment. "Um, sure, Mary, it's alright with me as long as it's alright with Anny's mom. But are you sure Anny will want to come?"

"Oh, yes, I already asked her" said Mary, turning away to put the spices back on the counter top and missing the odd smile on her mother's face.

"Okay, then, Mary. Go ahead and ask her while there's time."

Mary grabbed her coat and gloves and scarf and hat and put them on, then headed out the door. She met Anny, similarly bundled up, about halfway down the path to their house.

"Brr, it's cold out this morning" said Anny.

"Good" said Mary. "That means Mr. Erikson will be sitting by his fireplace, snoozing."

The two girls set off on the side path past the hedge-field to Mr. Erikson's farm. The wind sort of whistled through the brambles and it would have been much colder if not for the walk warming them up.

They finally came up to the back yard of Mr. Erikson's house where he had the gate in the fenced area where he kept his turkeys. They were pecking and scratching in the dirt and looked sort of bored, Mary thought.

She reached up to the heavy latch which was a little above her shoulder and pushed it up, while Anny pulled the pin from the holes in the latch. This was why she'd needed Anny or another student to come along. She couldn't hold up the latch and pull the pins out at the same time.

As she opened the gate up, a few of the turkeys looked up from their pecking then went back to it. But one was close to the gate and eyed them warily. They stepped back out of the way to see what he would do.

He looked at them for a moment, then looked through the gate at the open farmyard on the other side of it. He stepped toward the gate, walked through it and stopped for a moment, as if unsure of his freedom.

Then, with a soft "gobble", he took off trotting towards the woods at the edge of the farm.

The other turkeys were watching this and they also followed him out of the gate and towards the woods. Mary and Anny looked at each other with smiles on their faces, then they closed the gate and latched the pin. Then they ran back down the path to the edge of the hedge-field.

"Any minute now, they'll start gobbling and Mr. Erickson will come out and try to catch them" said Mary. "We'd better get back home."

"Okay, Mary. But what do we tell our moms? We're supposed to be over at each others' houses."

"Hmm." Mary thought for a moment. "Oh, let's just tell them that we changed our minds."

"Okay, let's do that."

So the girls split up and went along the paths back to their respective houses. Mary's mother was still in the kitchen, working on the crust for an apple pie. As she walked into the kitchen and began taking her coat and gloves off, Mary's mom said,

"What did Anny say about coming over?"

"Oh, she changed her mind."

"Oh, that's too bad. Okay, put your things up and then come help me with the pies, please."

Mary's dad came in a moment later from working in their goat barn, milking the dairy goats. As he took off his coat and things and laid them on the rack by the stove to dry, she could see his mustache had a slight bit of snow on it and Mary looked out the window to see big flakes coming down.

"I'm going to head over to Erickson's to pick out a turkey" Mary's dad said to her mom. "I'll call you when I've got one ready for plucking".

Mary was busy flattening out an apple pie crust with a rolling pin and didn't see that her mother noticed her smiling to herself when her dad mentioned the turkey. Her mother whispered something in her dad's ear and he went to use the phone.

"Mr. Erickson? I called to see if you were ready to let me come and pick out a turkey and … what? Really? Okay, I'll call a couple of people and we'll come and help you catch them."

He hung up the phone and turned to look at Mary's mom. "Hmm, it seems that all Erickson's turkeys got out somehow. I'm going to go get Almond and Fitzgerald to help me catch them. I'll be back later."

After her dad had put his outside clothes back on and left, Mary was humming to herself as she worked on the pie. Then Mary's mother finished with the pie she was filling and spoke as she laid the crust on top.

"Kind of odd that all the turkeys got out."

"Yes" replied Mary, trying not to look smug.

"Specially on Thanksgiving morning."

"Yes" said Mary. "Maybe Mr. Erickson better fix his gate latch."

"How do you know the gate latch had anything to do with it, Mary?" her mother asked sharply.

"Um... well... uh..." Mary's face turned red and she kind of scrunched it up, looking down at her pie. Suddenly releasing the turkeys didn't seem like such a great idea, after all.

"Mary, do you have something to say?" Her mother looked at her, closely.

Now, Mary was indeed The Mary That Wouldn't, but one of those things that she really wouldn't do, is lie. So after some hemming and hawing, her mother finally got the story out of her. And her mother called Anny's mother and Anny's mother got the story out of her.

All the turkeys were caught but not in time for dinner. So there were quite a few families and their children not too happy with Mary and Anny that particular Thanksgiving day.

Later that night, as Mary's mother went to tuck her into bed, Mary asked her,

"Was it really wrong to let the turkeys out?"

Mary's mother thought for a moment before she answered.

"Well, you or Anny could have been hurt if they got scared and tried to rush the gate. And lots of people went without turkey today because of what you two did. I think if you don't want to eat me- er, do something, that's fine. But I don't think you should stop other people from doing it. Do you?"

Mary looked down at her blanket, thoughtful for a moment, then looked up at her mother and replied,

"Hmmm. I like to sit on the pile of stones by Mr. Erickson's hedgerow and watch the trees and animals nearby. I wouldn't like it if someone stopped me from doing it. So, no, I don't think I should. Should I apologize to Mr. Erickson and everybody?"

"Well" said Mary's mother, "you can do that tomorrow. You've had enough to do for one day."

Mary got a kiss from her mother then snuggled down into the covers. Mary's mother walked out of the room and stopped at the door.

"Mary?"

"Yes, ma'am?"

"You know, it occurred to me that there have been holidays that some people try to get others to do things they don't want to do, either. So I think I might have a talk with your cousins about why you did what you did today, okay?"

She smiled and Mary understood that she'd have no problems not eating me- er, being full on holidays any more. She did feel kind of bad about what she did to Mr. Erickson and the other families and she would definitely apologize the next day.

She wouldn't do it next year. But, maybe, just maybe, she could think of something else to do to make sure she would not have to have turkey. She did, after all, have a whole year to plan...

What story collection of tales about an Island would be complete without a story about pirate treasure? And Moley, who loves stories about pirates, is right in the thick of things with his best friend, Jack, in the next tale.

The
Secret Cave

The Green Man
And The Dark

So... once upon a time, there was The Green Man. Not a Blue Man or an Orange Man or even a Purple Man but a Green Man. He wore only green shirts, green pants, green shoes, and

floppy green hats. Why only green, I don't know. I never thought to ask him in all the times I've talked to him.

I met him many times in the coffee shop where I go to when I want to drink coffee and write down my ideas. He told me other stories, about Pumpkin Jack and The Mary That Wouldn't and The Sawdust Wagon, all set in the Land of Fall, so when he came into the coffee shop that hot

summer day, I was curious to see if he
had any summer stories.

He slid into the booth across
from me and ordered his usual, green
tea, then asked me with a smile,

"Warm enough for you?"

Since I knew he really
preferred cooler weather, I knew it was
definitely warm enough for him.

"Yes, it is. I'm afraid it might
get too hot, especially for you."

"I'm not afraid. But Freckled
Moley was."

With that statement, off we
were again for another story about the
Land of Fall. Unlike almost all the
others, though, this one took place in
the short period of summer there.

We've talked before, you and I, about
the Land of Fall and how it's always
fall there. How it is usually chilly and
brisk mornings, shuffly dry leaves on

the sidewalk, pumpkins and tomatoes and corn waiting to be picked, crows cawing in the fields over the leftovers.

But though they are short, the Land does have other seasons. Mrs. Bobson, the grocer, and Mr. Fitzgerald, the vegetable farmer, get their seeds planted quickly in the spring. The school children enjoy snow forts and sliding down Crawberry Hill during the winter. They also like swimming on the beach near the fish shop in the summer, and that's when our story takes place.

On a warm Saturday late afternoon, Freckled Moley and his friend, Jack, were slowly walking around on the beach near the dock, looking for interesting shells and stones and whatever else they could find that caught their fancy.

Freckled Moley was called that because he had freckles on his face, freckles on his hands and arms, freckles on his legs. Jack often said he had freckles on his freckles.

Jack stooped down to pick up an interesting shell, a small spiral conch shell, and handed it to Moley.

"My dad says if you put it up to your ear, you can hear the ocean."

Moley looked doubtful but put it up to his ear and listened for a moment.

"I don't hear anything, except maybe my stomach growling."

Jack laughed and said,

"Yes, it's been a long time since lunch. Want to get something to eat at the fish-seller's shack today?"

"Sure" said Moley. "But we have to wash our hands afterward better than we did the last time. My mother made me scrub all the skin off my hands, almost, to get that fish smell out."

The boys laughed and turned around to walk back to the dock area where Mr. Almond's shack was sitting on the pier, way out on the dock. They liked to sit on the stools and eat while the seagulls squawked and swooped round and round overhead, waiting for the boys to drop something.

As they came up to the shop, Mr. Almond came out of the smoke room and saw them. He went to the sink, washed his hands and said,

"What can I do for you boys?"

"We'd like two fish sandwiches, Mr. Nut." The fish seller's last name was Almond but he asked everyone to call him Mr. Nut, which he thought was very funny.

He smiled and got the two boys their sandwiches. They took them to the end of the pier, a great oak wood platform for the fishermen and sat on the end, their legs dangling, as they unwrapped and ate their sandwiches while watching the sun sink lower in the west.

"Mrrgmg amgh mrrgff" said Jack, through a mouthful of fish, pointing at something farther down the beach from the pier.

"What?" asked Moley.

Jack swallowed his bite of sandwich and spoke again.

"Look at that pile of rocks along the far side past the boat launch. Isn't that a cave?"

"It kinda looks like it" said Moley, hesitating. "Why?"

"Let's go check it out. Just think of it! We're probably the first ones to go into it. Most people don't use that side of the boat launch."

"I don't know, Jack" said Moley. "You know I don't like dark places. And my mother wouldn't like it if we went in there. Remember when we got in trouble for going into the old abandoned Peterson House on the other side of the Island."

"Aw, come on" said Jack, obviously excited now at the idea. "We could get flashlights and just go in for a little ways. There might be pirate treasure in there!"

Jack knew if there was one way to get Moley to go with him, it was to mention pirate treasure. Moley was always checking books out of the school library or at Mr. Boot's bookshop on sea pirates and ship battles and having mock sword fights with Jack using old willow branches as their choice of weapons.

"Well, okay, if we get flashlights. But let's not stay too long, alright? Where are we going to get flashlights, though? If we go home, our parents won't let us back out to come to the beach. It's getting a little late."

Jack thought for a moment, then said,

"We could borrow them from Mr. Nut. We'll just tell him that we want them to look for shells since it's getting late. We'll drop the flashlights back off at his store on the way home."

"Okay" said Moley "but only for a little while."

Jack nodded and the two boys stood up from where they'd been sitting at the end of the pier, grabbed their fish sandwich papers and their empty bottles of juice and threw them in the trash barrel just to the side of the bench where Mr. Nut's sandwich customers sat.

"Mr. Nut?" Jack called and watched him come out from the back smoke room of the fish shop.

"Yes, boys, what can I do for you?"

"We wanted to look for some more shells on the beach but it's getting a little late. Can we borrow a couple of flashlights?"

Mr. Nut stood still and thought for a moment.

"Sure, boys, but bring them back when you're done. And be careful; the rocks on the beach can be slippery, even when you can see where you're stepping."

The two boys nodded, got their flashlights from Mr. Nut and put them in their pockets, then walked back off the pier to the beach area. They pulled out the flashlights and walked slowly down the beach, at first just pretending to look for shells.

But Moley found a small curly shell that was in good condition and Jack found a shell that was shaped like a skinny ice cream cone, the old-fashioned kind. They almost forgot about the cave, till they got near the opening.

The outside was shaped sort of like an arch, with moss and old seabirds' nests and dried grasses covering the rocks that formed the archway of the entrance.

Beach sand occasionally trickled down from rocks on the side of it where the tides and wind had originally blown it up there. The floor of the cave in the entrance looked dry enough, rocky with small pebbles and the occasional larger flat stone forming the surface.

"It looks a little spooky" said Moley timidly, as he turned on his flashlight and peered further into the cave.

"Nah, it's great, Moley" said Jack as he took a couple steps into the entrance. "We could find all kinds of stuff in here!"

Moley followed Jack further into the cave, promising himself that he'd only go 'for a little while'.

The original entrance went straight in and down at an angle that wasn't too steep, so the boys were able to look at the sights surrounding them in wonder. There were shells and fish bones and sea bird nests here and there, in the beginning.

But as they went farther, they saw less and less signs of the beach world outside the cave and more of the cave itself. The walls were mostly some sort of dark rock and white quartz crystals, covered with moss here and there and the occasional white toadstool popping up.

They scrambled down a short but steep incline and came to a room big enough to fit the whole fish-seller's shop into, with a few rocks almost as big as the boys themselves. The walls here were mostly a sort of white crystal, being far enough from the entrance to not get the mud and sand that the storms would bring. There were three passages branching out from this room.

"Which..." Moley whispered initially, then said again in a stronger voice,

"Which one should we try, Jack?"

Jack looked at the three passages. They all looked about the same to him, a little spooky, though he wasn't going to admit that to himself and certainly not to Moley.

"Let's try the center one, Moley" said Jack. "We can always come back if there's nothing there."

The boys walked on for a ways more, walking around boulders, occasionally hopping over small streams with white fish swimming in them, till they grew tired.

"Well, no treasure, Moley" said Jack. "We'd better go back but let's sit for a minute, I'm tired."

They were in a small room somewhat like the bigger chamber they'd seen before, but a little smellier and there seemed to be more sand and mud on the floor, too.

Suddenly, both boys heard a high-pitched squeaking sound. They looked fearfully at each other for a second then looked around the chamber but couldn't see anything.

Then a thought came to them at the same time. They both looked at each other and slowly turned their flashlights up toward the ceiling of the room.

Bats. Lots and lots and lots of bats. Bats covering the ceiling in humps and mounds. As the light hit them, they began to squeak even louder and started dropping down, flying everywhere in the small room and especially around the boys.

The boys jumped up and ran from the room down one of the passages, dodging the bats and the occasional rock as best they could. They'd gotten quite a bit away from the room and were just starting to slow down to stop when Jack tripped and fell, crying out in pain as he did so. He also dropped his flashlight and there was a tinkle of broken glass as the light abruptly went out.

"What's wrong, Jack?" asked Moley, shining his light over Jack laying on the ground while he held his ankle and grimaced in pain.

"I hurt my ankle really bad when I fell."

"Can you walk on it?"

Jack gingerly tried to put a small amount of pressure on the ankle and yelped, then stopped.

"Ouch! No, I can't, Moley."

"What are we going to do, Jack?"

"You'll have to go back and get help, Moley. Get our parents to come and get me. I can't walk and you can't carry me."

"But- but I'll have to take the flashlight. You'll be here in the dark, by yourself."

Jack swallowed and looked up fearfully at Moley.

"It's the only way, Moley. We have no choice. You remember how to get out?"

Moley nodded, though he wasn't quite exactly sure of the way. But he knew Jack depended on him and even though Jack had said before that he wasn't afraid of the dark, Moley knew this was a little different.

"I'll go get help, Jack. I'll be back. I will."

The two boys looked at each other and then Jack nodded. Moley turned around and went back hurriedly toward the room where the bats were. As he came to the room entrance, he slowed down and peeked in but the bats appeared to be either all settled down or gone.

Just to make sure he didn't disturb them again, he made sure he pointed his flashlight only at the floor as he went across the room to the other exit. He wound his way among the twist and turns of the rocks and passages, feeling not totally sure that he was going the right way until he came into the big room.

He stood there for a moment in the opening, trying to figure out a way to make sure when the parents came back through that they could find the right entrance. Then an idea came to him, one he'd read about in his pirate books. He piled up a bunch of loose rocks and pebbles in the center of the passageway back to Jack. That way, when they came back through, they'd know the right one to pick. He scrambled through the large room, aware always in his head that Jack was back there, alone, in the dark, waiting for help.

Finally, Moley found the exit to the cave arch and ran through it out onto the beach. The sun was very low on the horizon, the sunset making pretty purple and orange clouds in the sky. But he didn't have time to look at those.

He ran from the beach out onto the pier, hoping to find Mr. Nut still in his fish-seller's shop as that was the closest grownup he knew to find. Mr. Nut was standing in the large open doorway to the shop and just reaching up to close the main door, sort of a garage-like door that slid down.

"Mr. Nut, Mr. Nut!" Moley exclaimed as he ran onto the pier. "Help, help!"

Mr. Nut turned around in surprise and saw Moley running along the pier up to him.

"What's the matter, Moley?"

"Jack's fallen in the cave and has hurt himself and he can't walk and -" Moley stopped, in tears and out of breath.

"Calm down and catch your breath, Moley. Then tell me what happened."

Moley told Mr. Nut about the cave, their flashlights, the bats and Jack hurting his ankle. So Mr. Nut went to his phone in the shop and called Jack's parents and Moley's mom. He let her know that they would need Moley to help find Jack but that she could meet Jack's parents at the shop and to wait there for them.

He also called Mrs. Durham, the only doctor on the Island, and Mr.

Fitzgerald, the farmer who was also a volunteer fireman, to help in the rescue.

The two rescuers quickly arrived with extra flashlights. They and Mr. Nut followed as Moley led them down along the beach to the cave. It was just barely big enough for the grownups to walk through, stooping a little in some spots.

They came to the large chamber and Moley pointed out the rock pile he'd made to let them know which passage to take.

"That was a good idea, Moley" said Dr. Durham as she walked across the chamber. "Otherwise, we might become lost ourselves."

As they came to the bat room, Moley slowed down again but there still didn't seem to be any bats in it, for which he was thankful.

He started calling out,
"Jack, Jack!" as he went along, waiting
a moment each time to hear a reply.
Finally, he got back a faint
"I'm here!"

They found Jack sitting up
against one wall of the passageway
where he'd scooted, his pained leg
stretched out in front of him. Dr.
Durham set her bag down next to his
ankle and said,

"Let's look at this, shall we?
Did you fall, Jack?"

"Yes, Dr. Durham. I slipped as
I was running."

Jack bit his lip for a moment,
tears forming in his eyes as she used a
pair of scissors to cut off the shoe,
revealing his bruised and swollen
ankle.

As the doctor worked on his
ankle, Jack looked up at Moley.

"I knew you'd come, Moley. I just knew it. Even though you're afra-" Jack broke off with a grunt as the doctor probed his ankle with her fingers. Moley looked down at the ground for a moment, a lump suddenly in his throat.

"It doesn't appear to be broken, Jack" said the doctor, finally. "I'll put a splint on it so it doesn't wobble around and Mr. Fitzgerald can carry you out. Mr. Nut can help if he gets tired. I don't want any weight put on that ankle."

Mr. Nut looked down at Moley for a moment, about to ask him why the boys were in the cave. But Moley looked so miserable and sad about Jack's ankle being hurt that he decided to wait until later.

"Finished" said Dr. Durham as she wrapped up the last bit of ankle.

"Here's a couple of aspirin to help with the pain till we get you home, Jack".

Jack took the aspirin and swallowed them with the water from the water bottle Dr. Durham kept in her bag, then stood up on his good leg, with her help. Mr. Fitzgerald picked him up and carried him down the passage.

They traveled through the bat room and the big room and finally back out onto the beach where they met Jack and Moley's parents, who had been unwilling to wait on the pier.

Jack was turned over to his father, who carried him back along the beach. Moley was hugged by his mom, who didn't scold him too much for going into the cave with Jack. She saw how bad he felt already and figured he had learned his lesson.

The two boys were the talk of the schoolhouse for the next day or so, telling of their adventures. They knew they'd been lucky, though, and decided that maybe, just maybe, a pirate's cave was a little more exciting in real life than what it appeared to be in books.

The tales in this book have been about many things but mostly centering on family and friendship and that's why I wanted to save this next tale for last: A Giant's Belt.

A
Giant's
Belt

The Green Man

And Loss

The coffee shop was almost full that day but I was too sad to notice much of the usual clamor. I sat, staring out the window, an occasional tear running down my cheek and sniffling. The cold rainy autumn afternoon seemed to match my mood perfectly. Even the diner, as full as it was, was quieter than normal.

As I stared, I noticed something moving in the steady drizzle. At first it seemed like a vague shape, I wasn't sure what it was. Then it finally resolved itself into the Green Man. He seemed to dissolve into being slowly, rather than just suddenly appear. I watched his progress along the street. As he came closer, he saw me looking at him through the cafe's big front window and waved slightly, then looked puzzled when I didn't return the wave.

He came in the door of the cafe, shook off the rain, slapped his floppy green leather hat against his green raincoat and came over to my table. The regular waitress, used to our habits by now, brought him a hot pot of water, a bunch of green tea bags and a small carafe of black coffee for me. He slid into the seat at the booth across from me, waited until the waitress had set down our water and coffee and then he spoke.

"You look a bit sad today" he said in quiet tones.

"I am" I said, still looking out the window at the rain. "I just received some sad news about my father."

"Can I tell you a story?" He asked hesitantly, as if he didn't want to break into my sorrow.

"Sure" I replied, turning to look at him and trying to smile. "Is it a sad story?"

"It is" he said. "But it's a good one, too."

The Island is a beautiful place. It is mostly forest and natural clearings. It has a few small quaint villages, farms and roads that are often meant to walk slowly upon, rather than travel quickly anywhere.

Freckled Moley and Jack were walking one day along just such a road, from Jack's house where they'd been playing to Scarecrow Corners, where the small dusty bookstore of Mr. Boot was located. The boys were best friends and their best place to go on the Island on a Saturday morning was to Mr. Boot's shop.

Mr. Boot was a rather roundish person. He wore roundish spectacles and had a pair of enormous round-bottomed mutton chop sides to his mustache. He was also rather round in body, being almost as big around as he was tall, which wasn't that tall. His shop sort of matched his person, with round windows in the front of it and two round lamps outside his shop for when it got dark.

His friend and assistant, Turner Jake, was just the opposite of Mr. Boot. He was called Turner Jake because he liked to read the books that were sold and traded at Mr. Boot's shop. He could read the pages almost as fast as he could turn them and it took him almost no time at all to go through a book. He was taller than Mr. Boot was round, had a skinny beard on his skinny face and long hair tied into a skinny ponytail going down his back.

Jack and Moley liked Mr. Boot's shop
for a couple of good reasons. First, he
wasn't so picky as other shop owners
seemed to be on the mainland. He
would let you browse among the books,
take your time and not rush you. You
could wander there around the shelves,
you could take a cup of hot water from
the teapot on the wood stove and make
tea or hot cocoa, you could just chat
with Mr. Boot or Turner Jake,
whomever happened to be in the shop
at the time. The other reason they liked
Mr. Boot's shop better was MissV.
MissV was Mr. Boot's dog.

No one, not even Mr. Boot, was quite
sure what type of dog MissV was, other
than that she was rather the largest
rather furry and rather friendly type
that anyone had seen on the Island. She
easily came up to Jack's dad's waist in
height and had long fluffy brown hair
that was black in spots and white in
others. She wore a wide purple nylon

collar with her name engraved on a small metal disk that hung on it. She had been a part of Mr. Boot's shop ever since Jack could remember, with her huge furry wagging tail (which was occasionally Dangerous To The Bookshelves) and her huge slobbery tongue when giving kisses, her favorite activity.

She had grown a little stiffer, a little slower, a little more thoughtful, as Jack's dad was wont to say, over the years but still enjoyed the visits from the Island's schoolchildren. She liked to hang out mostly near Mr. Boot's small (and of course, round) wood stove in the corner, wagging her tail when customers came in and enjoying the pets she got as part of her regal due. Mr Boot would, every Sunday, take MissV on a slow walk around the Island.

He would stop at the fish-seller's shop on the pier and get his dried haddock for his Monday night suppers, he'd stop at Dr. Durham's office in case she had any small children that needed comforting by MissV's rather large and friendly tail, he'd stop at all kinds of places and talk to all kinds of people.

People liked to talk to him, of course, but they liked to talk to MissV as well, scratching her behind the ears, the younger children taking short rides on her wide back, thumping her sides while saying "Good Girl" and seeing if she'd turn down this time the dog treats everyone seemed to keep around on Sundays, even if they didn't own a dog.

He was also in the habit of taking his usual lunch of pickled bologna slices and a large chunk of hard sharp cheddar cheese and a couple of pieces of crusty bread. Sometimes he'd feed the bread or the remains of it to the birds that congregated on or near the bench outside his shop while MissV lay on the ground next to him and snoozed.

Jack and Moley crossed the small mortar and stone bridge that led to the main street in Scarecrow Corners and turned to the right, where Mr. Boot's shop was located.

It was a wooden storefront, with new books always portrayed on the movable shelves in the large round window on the left and his loaner books, ones that had been in the store for a while and hadn't been sold or ones that had been returned, always portrayed in the large round window on the right.

Normally, there was a big "Come On In, The Reading's Fine!" sign hanging in the window of the door to the shop. But this time, it was flipped around and Mr. Boot was backing out of the door, his shop key in his hand hanging from the round ring he carried such keys upon.

"Mr. Boot, why are you closing up so early? It's not even noon yet" asked Jack as they came up to the shop door.

He turned around and the boys saw with some surprise that there appeared to be tears in his eyes. He looked down at them for a moment, smiled a little sadly and said,

"I won't be open today, boys. MissV has... MissV is..." His breath caught in a small sob for a second, then he continued.

"MissV is no longer with us."

"What?" the boys exclaimed together, looking at each other. MissV had been there longer on the Island than they had, this couldn't be true!

He saw the look on their faces and continued.

"I'm sorry, boys. There are things I must do. There are preparations that I must make and..."

Moley interrupted with,

"Can we help?"

Mr. Boot looked as if at first he was going to say no, then changed his mind.

"Actually, yes, boys. If anyone who wanted to could... could find their way to my house tomorrow about noon, just outside of town here, by the large willow tree, I think that would be a good thing."

He finished locking the door, nodded to the boys then walked off down the street, his normal bouncy walk replaced by a steady tread that seemed as if he were trying to shake off his sadness.

Jack looked at Moley for a moment, then said,

"We need to call everyone. Lots of people liked MissV and like Mr. Boot and Turner Jake."

"I agree, Jack. Let's go home and start calling people."

The boys headed off to their houses. When they got home, they told their parents what had happened at the bookstore. Jack's dad hugged him and Moley's mom hugged him. It seemed a good time for hugs. They began calling people, starting with The Mary That Wouldn't (but this time, she would) and her friend, Anima, and their friends and their friends' friends till soon, most of the people on the Island knew.

The next day dawned sunny and clear but cool. Mr. Boot sat in the front bay window of his cottage, holding the large purple nylon collar, remembering things as he looked out the window overlooking the small pond on the side of his house and the giant willow tree that seemed to spread out over the whole property, it was so big. He'd been sitting there, all morning, missing MissV's thumping tail and dreading what was to come, turning the collar back and forth in his hands. But finally, it was about an hour before noon and he knew it was time. As he stepped out of his front door, Turner Jake opened his front gate and walked into the yard.

"Pretty morning for such a day, isn't it?" he said, watching Mr. Boot's face.

"Yes. Yes, it is" said Mr. Boot. "MissV would have..." he choked up and couldn't continue. Turner Jake gently held his shoulder for a moment, then turned toward the willow tree. When he did, Mr. Boot could see the shovel he'd brought.

They took turns digging, as it was kind of hard, rocky soil they were digging in and even with the cool weather, it was warming work. Finally, it was done. The mound of earth had a wooden post planted in it with the large purple collar nailed to the front of it. They both sat down to rest on wooden lawn chairs under the willow that Mr. Boot used, in happier times, to read while sitting in and enjoying the day.

"Would you like.. would you like to say anything, Mr. Boot?" asked Turner Jake.

"I would" said a voice behind them. They turned and looked and there was a small crowd of people standing there, with occasional stragglers coming up the lane and making it bigger. There was Dr. Durham and her daughter, Samantha, and Pumpkin Jack and his parents, and The Mary That Wouldn't and all her brothers and sisters and her parents, and Freckled Moley and his mom and Mr. Nut, the fish seller and so many that it seemed as if half the Island had shown up that morning.

"Why- " a lump seemed to catch in Mr. Boot's throat and he had some trouble in swallowing it. "Why, sure, you can say something. Who wants to go first?"

There was a pause for a moment, then The Mary stepped forward and looked down at the patch of turned earth and the purple collar on the post.

"I always liked it when she- "she paused, sniffled, then went on, "when she would lick my face and make me giggle, even though I would pretend to scold her."

"I always liked her bark" said Moley, stepping forward as well and standing next to Mary. "I was a little less afraid of... afraid, when she was around."

As each of the Island's people and their kids came forward and said what they remembered best about MissV, the memories caught up with Mr. Boot and he began silently crying, tears running down his face and hiding for a bit in his muttonchops till they overran those and began dripping off his chin. Mr. Nut's feeding a piece of smoked cod to MissV every time Mr. Boot came along the pier to the fish seller's shop, Dr. Durham talking about how MissV made kids feel better, even if they had to get a shot, Mr. Grimbleson talking about how he could teach the younger children to count by how many barks MissV would make when she hung around outside the classroom and wanted the kids to come out and play, all the memories. It all seemed too much to Mr. Boot and he hung his head, sniffling, till he felt a small hand slip into his.

"Mr. Boot?" He looked up and standing in front of him was the black-haired wiry-headed Tommy, The Mary That Wouldn't's youngest brother, barely in school. "Mr. Boot, I know it won't bring MissV back but I want to give you a hug. Can I?"

He nodded emphatically. "Yes, Tommy. A hug would be great." So Tommy gave him a hug. Then one by one, the people there came up and also gave him a hug. The last one, the farmer Ericksen, hugged him and then said,

"When you have time, come and see me tomorrow."

Mr. Boot nodded miserably and sat, lost in thought, his shoulders slumped, as the crowed slowly began to filter away. Finally, there was no one left but him and Turner Jake.

"Take the day off tomorrow, Jake" said Mr. Boot in a tired voice. "I don't feel like opening the store."

"Yessir" said Turner Jake. "Are you going over to Mr. Ericken's tomorrow?"

Mr. Boot sighed, stood up, said, "I don't know, Jake. I just don't know", and walked slowly into the cottage, quietly closing the door behind him. Turner Jake stood there for a moment, staring at the door, then he looked down at the bare patch on the ground. A wistful look came across his face, he nodded once, leaned the shovel over his shoulder and began the walk back into the village.

The next day, Mr. Boot was just cleaning up from his breakfast when he heard a knock at the door. 'I wonder who that could be, this early?' he thought as he went to answer it.

When he opened the door, there stood Turner Jake and Mr. Ericksen, who was holding a large burlap bag.

"Morning" said Mr. Boot. "What can I do for-"

"It's not what you can do for us, it's what we can do for you" said Turner

Jake as they walked past Mr. Boot into the neat cottage. A sudden yip coming from the bag gave Mr. Boot a clue as to what they were up to.

"Look" he began, "I appreciate the thought but it's a bit too soon to -"

"Well, here's the problem" interrupted Mr. Ericksen. "This fella's mother got sick and she can't take care of him any more. I realize it's soon but if you could help me out for just a little while, I-"

A brown nose appeared out of the bag's opening, followed by a weirdly purple and pink spotted tongue, followed by an even weirder looking puppy. It was wiry-haired, with patches of odd color on it, a white patch over its left eye and what looked like spotted brown and black and white wiry fur over the rest of it, even on its huge paws. It wiggled out of Mr. Ericksen's bag, dropped to the floor and began to wander around and explore the cottage.

"Yes, well, that's all well and good but _"

"Please" said Turner Jake. "Just for a couple of days."

Mr. Boot sighed and looked down at the puppy, who looked up at him as if to say, 'Hey, what are you doing in my cottage?'

"Well, okay, if it's only for a couple of days."

Turner Jake and Mr. Ericksen hid their smiles mostly successfully and they walked out of the cottage, Mr. Ericksen agreeing to take the puppy back as soon as Mr. Boot was done with it.

"Hmm" said Mr. Boot to the puppy, once they were gone. "Now what do we do, my young canine friend?"

The puppy promptly answered him by lifting his leg and wetting the newspaper that had fallen to the floor when Mr. Boot had gotten up to answer the door.

'Oh well' thought Mr. Boot as he picked up the paper and wagged his finger scoldingly at the puppy, 'at least he did it on the paper'.

It was a whole week, not just one day, before Mr. Boot opened up his shop again. Jack and Moley came, that day being a Saturday again and no school.

When they walked into the shop, the puppy, who'd been laying on the floor by the stove, not in MissV's spot but close, yipped once at them, then promptly fell back asleep.

"He seems to be doing okay" said Moley to Mr., Boot as they walked up to the counter.

"Yes, Moley, I think he'll do rather well here."

"Have you thought of a name for him yet?" asked Jack.

"Well..." said Mr. Boot, slowly. "He does appear to be rather patchy on his outer surfaces so I believe I shall call him Patch. How's that for a name, Patch? Do you like it?" he asked the puppy.

And the puppy just grinned.

Author's Note: I hope you, Illustrious Reader, liked reading these stories as much as I liked writing them. I love the idea of wandering the lanes, farms, villages and hedgerows of the Island. I enjoy my conversations with Jack and Mary and Uncle Robert and Mr. Boot and the rest. I've thumped MissV's sides and called her "Good Girl" and laughed at Patch's antics.

I love the idea of wandering the Island, of being allowed into the lives of the people who live on there. It's a special privilege for me and one that I wanted to share with you. You never know what you're going to find there.

There will soon be translations made available in Spanish and French. I hope to add more in the future. I'm sure I'll be able to write more of them, though. After all, who knows when I'll get another visit from the Green Man?

Made in the USA
Las Vegas, NV
26 July 2022

52224215R00094